NINJA MEERKATS

Read all the Ninja Meerkats Adventures!

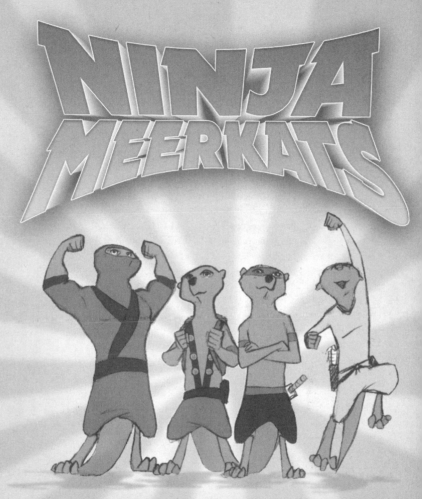

NINJA MEERKATS

THE EYE OF THE MONKEY

GARETH P. JONES

SQUARE
FISH

NEW YORK

SQUARE FISH

An Imprint of Macmillan

ISBN 978-1-250-01665-2

Originally published in Great Britain by Stripes Publishing
First Square Fish Edition: January 2013
Square Fish logo designed by Filomena Tuosto
mackids.com

2 4 6 8 10 9 7 5 3 1

For Aled and Owain Lewis
~ *G P J*

I believe it was the great meerkat philosopher Booda Steachings who said:

A red traffic light means very little to the color-blind meerkat.

These words of wisdom would have been the first of many, had Booda not met his end under a twenty-ton truck one fateful night. It turned out he was putting his theory to the test.

"But what has this to do with the story I am about to read?" I hear you cry. You may well ask. But I will not answer . . . for I have already forgotten the question. And, indeed, what I am doing altogether.

So instead, allow me to introduce you to the Clan of the Scorpion . . .

Four ninja meerkats, all powerful
warriors, ever ready to leave their home in
the Red Desert and save the world from our
deadly enemy, the Ringmaster.

Jet Flashfeet: a superfast
ninja whose only fault is craving
the glory he so
richly deserves.

Bruce "the muscle"
Willowhammer: the
strongest of the gang,
though in the brain race, he lags somewhat
behind.

Donnie Dragonjab: a brilliant
mind, inventor, and master of
gadgets.

Chuck Cobracrusher: his
clear leadership has saved the
others' skins more times
than I care to remember.

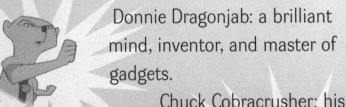

Oh, and me, Grandmaster One-Eye: as old and wise as the sand dunes themselves.

In this adventure, the Clan journey to India to help out an old friend of mine, known as the Delhi Llama. He was a fearsome fighter in his day and it was he who introduced me to the poetry of Alan Gwidge-Smith. I will leave you with one of his poems:

When it rains, I do often wish
That I had a big umbrella.
But when the sun shines in the sky
I'm happy as any fella.

Enjoy the story of . . .
THE EYE OF THE MONKEY.

CHAPTER ONE

THE DELHI LLAMA

The streets of Old Delhi can be a confusing place for newcomers. They are noisy, dusty, and jam-packed with cars, vans, rickshaws, bicycles, street sellers, tourists, and cows, which are allowed to wander anywhere they wish, getting in everyone's way. This can also be said of the tourists, although the cows tend to take fewer photos.

On this particular morning, there were also four meerkats who were enjoying the hustle and bustle because it allowed them to walk unnoticed through the streets.

"I still don't understand where we're going," said Bruce.

"We've been through this," said Donnie, who was wearing a hefty backpack full of gadgets, disguises, and inventions. "We have come to see Smo Ka, the Delhi Llama."

"Smo who the what?" said Bruce.

"Smo Ka, the Delhi Llama. He's a kung fu legend," said Jet. "He invented the Lightning Spin Kick, a kick so fast if you blink, you'll miss it. I've never managed it, but I'm hoping he'll give me some tips. He also wrote *The Four Elements of Kung Fu*. I've brought along my copy to have it signed." Jet held up a well-thumbed book from his collection of martial arts manuals.

"Many years ago, Smo Ka trained with our own Grandmaster One-Eye," said Chuck. "That is how he came to hear of us and why he requested our help."

"But what does he need our help with?"
asked Bruce.

"That we do not know," Chuck replied.
"All we've been given is his address. He will
explain when we see him."

The Clan passed a street vendor with
a large stack of samosas.

Bruce's stomach rumbled.
"Can we stop for a quick
bite?" he asked.

"No, Smo is expecting us," replied Chuck.

"But what about breakfast? All I've eaten since we left the Red Desert were those sugar-coated ants' antennae," moaned Bruce. "And doesn't my mom always says it's important to try the local food?"

"Your mom has never left her burrow in her whole life," said Jet.

"Exactly. She always eats locally," replied Bruce.

Donnie rolled his eyes. "All right, I'll get you one of those samosas." From his backpack, he pulled out a device made from a fishing rod and a pair of tweezers. He cast the line, sending the tweezers flying into the air. They latched onto a samosa on top of the pile.

"Nice one, Donnie," Bruce cheered.

But the flying snack did not go
unnoticed by the street vendor. "My
samosa has sprouted wings," he cried.

"Donnie, like the elephant who puts on a
bikini and enters a beauty contest, you are
drawing too much attention to yourself,"
said Chuck sternly. "Release the samosa."

"Sorry," said Donnie. He reeled in the line
and dropped Bruce's snack on the ground.

Bruce reached for the samosa, but Chuck grabbed his arm. "No, Bruce. Quickly, everyone. Down this alley." As the meerkats hurried down the quiet side street, Chuck turned to Donnie. "We are all grateful for your gadgets, but please remember—a ninja meerkat moves like a shadow through the streets. He does not steal samosas with a fishing rod."

Suddenly, Chuck stopped outside a ramshackle shed that looked like it was two gusts of wind away from being a pile of firewood. "We're here," he said.

"This can't be right," said Jet. "A legend like the Delhi Llama should live in a palace, not a shed. We must have the wrong address."

"A legend like the Delhi Llama would not care for things such as palaces," Chuck replied.

"Why's he called the Delhi Llama
anyway?" asked Bruce.

"I'll give you a clue," said Donnie.
"He lives here in Delhi and . . ." He paused
and looked at his friend.

"And what?" asked Bruce.

"Honestly, Bruce," said Donnie. "You are
a brave, strong, and skillful ninja, but
sometimes I wonder how you even manage
to get dressed in the morning."

Chuck banged on the door three times.

"Please enter," spoke a voice from within.

Bruce pushed open the door and they stepped inside. The interior of the shed was even more rundown than the outside, with little more for comfort than a bed of straw and a bowl of water. A battered notebook and a pot of ink lay next to the bed, but there was no sign of the kung fu legend himself.

"Hello? Smo Ka, sir?" said Jet.

"You may call me Smo." The voice made all four meerkats jump. It seemed to come from right in front of them.

"He's invisible," gasped Bruce.

"Not at all," said the voice. "I am merely standing behind you."

The meerkats turned to find a llama with dreadlocks standing in the doorway.

"How did you do that?" Jet asked.

"Years of practice. The ability to throw one's voice can be useful. It can convince an enemy he is surrounded, when in fact he only faces one llama," Smo replied.

"Oh! He's a *llama* that lives in *Delhi. That's* why he's called the Delhi Llama!" Bruce exclaimed.

"Very perceptive, Master Willowhammer," said Smo.

"How do you know my name?" asked Bruce.

"Grandmaster One-Eye has told me all about you. You are the legendary Clan of the Scorpion: Bruce "the muscle" Willowhammer, with the strength of eleven lions; Donnie Dragonjab—inventor, engineer, innovator; Chuck Cobracrusher, a wise and noble leader; and, of course, Jet Flashfeet, one of the most talented ninjas of his generation."

"I am thrilled to meet you, sir," said Jet. "I have read *The Four Elements of Kung Fu* many times. Would you do me the honor of signing my copy?"

"How kind of you, Master Flashfeet," said Smo. "Of course I will."

The llama took the book in his mouth and crossed the room, moving with a limp in his left hind leg. He lifted his front right hoof, dipped it in the pot of ink and carefully scribbled his name inside the book.

"Mr. Ka, sir, what is it that you need our assistance with?" asked Chuck.

"Please, call me Smo. Have you ever heard of the Eye of the Monkey?"

Chuck nodded. "It is an emerald which is said to give whoever possesses it the power of Infinite Protection."

"What does that mean?" asked Donnie.

"It means whoever has the jewel cannot be harmed," said Chuck. "The sharpest blade aimed at them will snap like a twig; the fastest bullet will bounce off their skin; even a bomb would be as harmless as a petal landing on their head."

"Sounds amazing!" said Jet.

"Indeed. And I believe it may be about to fall into the wrong hands," Smo replied.

"But its whereabouts have been kept secret for centuries," said Chuck, frowning.

Smo nodded. "This is true. But a contact of mine has heard that someone has learned of its hiding place and is looking for a thief to steal it. My contact also revealed that the person we seek wears a top hat and travels with a circus."

"The Ringmaster," Donnie said with a scowl.

"Precisely," said Smo.

"Then, we have no time to lose," said Chuck. "We must get to the emerald ahead of the thief. Smo, where is the Eye of the Monkey hidden?"

"Tell no one, but the jewel is in a secret temple near the city of Agra," the llama replied. "I shall take you there."

"But why do you need us at all?" asked Jet. "Are you not the kung fu legend who single-hoofedly defeated the five vipers of Varanasi?"

Smo chuckled. "Yes, but I had four fully working limbs back then, while the vipers didn't have a leg to stand on."

"But you invented the Lightning Spin Kick!" protested Jet.

"So I did," said Smo sadly. "Yet I've not performed it since I injured my leg. No, for this mission, I need the assistance of a brilliant leader, an inventive genius, an unstoppable forcc, and a dynamic fighter."

"Then look no further. The Clan of the Scorpion is at your service," said Chuck. "We will set off immediately."

"Ninja-boom!" cried Jet.

CHAPTER TWO

THE RIDDLE
OF THE TEMPLE

Every morning, thousands of humans travel through Delhi Station. But in the crowd on this particular morning, there was also an elderly llama pulling a trailer. And hidden inside were the ninja meerkats.

"How come we were able to walk around yesterday, but today we're cooped up in here?" grumbled Jet.

"Yesterday, we had no idea of our mission," said Chuck. "Today, we know who we face. If we were seen with the Delhi Llama, word might get back to the Ringmaster."

"Curse this wretched leg!" Smo
muttered. "We're going to miss our train!"
He hurried over to the platform, jolting the
cart along behind him, and arrived just as
the train to Agra began to pull out of the
station. "We've missed it!" he cried.

"Not yet, we haven't," replied Chuck,
leaping out and unhooking the trailer.
"Ninja meerkats, we have a train to catch!"

In most train stations in most countries, the sight of four meerkats running at full speed along a platform closely followed by a llama would have caused something of a stir. Such is the wonderfully chaotic nature of Delhi Station that, even as they barged past people selling hot chai and spicy biriyani, barely an eyebrow was raised.

The train was picking up speed as the meerkats approached the end of the platform. As they drew level with the last carriage, they leaped, one after the other, onto the ladder at the back of the train and clambered up onto the roof.

"Jump!" Chuck cried to Smo, who was struggling to keep up with the train.

"Can't," Smo wheezed. "Too weak."

"To conquer your weaknesses, you must remember your strengths!" Jet called out to the llama.

A look of steely determination crossed Smo's face. He put on a burst of speed, then threw himself at the ladder and clambered up onto the roof.

"I haven't run that fast in years!" panted Smo.

Chuck turned to Jet. "Those were wise words," he said.

"They are Smo's words," Jet replied.

The llama nodded. "It is the title of the final chapter in my book. You are right, Jet. I have allowed my injury to hold me back too long." He bowed to Jet in thanks.

A couple of hours later, the train arrived at Agra. Smo led the meerkats out of the city into the dry desert-like landscape beyond.

"Where is this temple?" asked Chuck, after they'd been walking for almost an hour in the growing heat of the day.

"At the base of a waterfall, in the center of a jungle," replied Smo.

"A waterfall and a jungle in this place?" Donnie snorted. "Looks like it rains here even less than it does back home."

"It is a secret oasis, unknown to most," replied Smo. "The water comes from an underground river. It's not far now."

He led them on, up a gently sloping hill. When they reached the top, Donnie gasped. For there far below, concealed by the surrounding hills, lay a lush green valley. At its heart stood a rocky outcrop, and a waterfall that splashed into a clear pool.

Smo led them down to the waterfall. A huge evergreen tree with spiky leaves stood beside it. Behind the tree was a stone door cut into the rock face and decorated with an elaborate carving of a monkey.

"Behind this door, it is said, is the temple that holds the Eye of the Monkey," Smo told them.

"Let us hope we have made it in time," said Chuck. "How do we get in?"

"I'm afraid I do not know," the llama admitted.

"Don't worry, I'll get it open," said Bruce. He took a long run up, then charged at the door . . . but bounced straight off it.

"I fear this door will not yield even to one as strong as you," said Smo.

"I've got a skeleton key that will open any door," said Donnie.

"A useful device no doubt, but one which requires a keyhole," Smo pointed out.

"So my Air-Key Open Palm Move won't be of any use either," said Jet. "Hang on, there's something carved into the rock here. What language is that?"

Smo squinted at the lettering. "It is
written in the ancient language of Sanskrit,
but I can translate it." He pulled out a pair
of reading glasses from inside his robe
and placed them on the end of his snout,
then said:

Use the puzzle to open the door,
To enter the temple you need four.
Three down gets one across,
If the three let go, it's the other one's
wash.

"What does that mean?" asked Bruce.
"It's a riddle," said Donnie.
Chuck stroked his chin and looked
around. His eyes rested on the nearby tree.
"This is a monkey puzzle tree. Perhaps it is
the puzzle the poem refers to."
"How about the next line? 'To enter

the temple you need four.' Four what?"
said Jet.

"I believe the clue to that is in the
third line of the puzzle," said Chuck.
"'Three down gets one across.' It must
mean that it takes four to enter the
temple," said Chuck. "Three have to do
something while one crosses the
threshold. But what?"

"Look here," said Donnie, who was
examining the tree more closely. "There's
something strange about these three
branches. They're not actually growing out
of the tree. They've been chopped off, then
reattached—see? They're connected to
some kind of mechanism using vines."

"That's it!" said Chuck. "Three of us
must pull down these branches to open
the door, while the other one enters
the temple."

"What about the last line of the riddle?" asked Jet. "'If the three let go, it's the other one's wash.'"

"I suppose it's about what happens if we release the branches while the other one is still inside," said Chuck. "But we do not need to worry about that. Bruce, Jet, and I will hold the branches while Donnie and Smo go inside to check on the Eye."

"Why Donnie? As the fastest, I should go in," Jet protested.

"No, Jet, I fear this temple holds yet more monkey business that will be better suited to Donnie's gadget know-how than your fighting skills," replied Chuck. "And Smo understands the local culture better than any of us."

"The rhyme says only one should enter," said Smo. "Would it not be dangerous if two go?"

"If Donnie rides on your back, it will be as if you are one," replied Chuck.

"So we've just got to hang around here like a bunch of bananas while he has all the fun?" Jet grumbled.

"It's a monkey puzzle tree," said Donnie. "So you're really more like a bunch of monkey nuts."

"Yeah? Well maybe this monkey nut will let go of his branch so you can find out what the last line of the riddle means!"

"You will do no such thing," said Chuck. "Donnie, you've got your cell phone—keep in contact."

Donnie nodded.

"Clan of the Scorpion!" said Chuck. "Take your positions and on my count, grab the branches. One . . . two . . . three. Now!"

Chuck, Jet, and Bruce jumped up and grabbed the three branches, pulling them down as hard as they could.

"Ow, these needles are sharp,"
complained Bruce.

There was a thud from behind the stone
door, then slowly it creaked open.

"That's neat," said Donnie. He peered into the tunnel. "Looks dark in there—lucky I brought this." He rooted around in his backpack and produced what looked like a child's bicycle helmet with a flashlight strapped to the front. He popped it on his head, then hopped onto Smo's back.

"Tread carefully," said Chuck.

Donnie switched on the flashlight as they entered the tunnel. It smelled musty and damp, and grew steadily darker and colder as Smo ventured further inside, following the passageway as it twisted and turned deep inside the rock.

Donnie's keen eyes scanned their surroundings. "There are engravings of monkeys on the walls," he pointed out.

"Monkeys are sacred in India," Smo explained. "Perhaps this temple was built to worship them."

They turned another corner and found themselves in a cavernous chamber. Donnie shone his flashlight around and gasped. There in front of them was a huge statue of a blue monkey sitting cross-legged, and wearing strings of black pearls around its neck, and a gold crown on its head. "Wow. That's one big monkey."

"It is Hanuman, the Hindu monkey god," Smo spoke in hushed tones.

Donnie examined the statue's face. One of the monkey's eyes was painted green, but the other was empty, as though something had been removed from it. "We've been beaten to it!" cried Donnie. "The thief has come and gone!"

"But how could anyone have climbed up so high?" said Smo.

"With that," said Donnie, pointing out a coiled rope on the floor.

Suddenly, a loud bang echoed along the tunnel and around the chamber.

"What was that?" whispered Smo.

"I fear that Jet has got bored and let go of his branch," said Donnie anxiously. "And I think that was the sound of the door slamming shut, locking us inside. But it's not all bad news."

"It isn't?" asked Smo.

"No. At least we'll get to find out what the last line of the riddle means."

"'If the three let go, it's the other one's wash,'" Smo remembered. Then he added, "Isn't that the sound of water?"

"Ah! So the door closes, triggering a mechanism that redirects the waterfall through the temple," said Donnie. "Clever! But don't worry, I have just the thing." He reached into his backpack and riffled around. "Now, where is it?"

The sound of rushing water grew louder.

"Haste would be no bad thing. Llamas are not natural swimmers," said Smo.

"Inflatable hat . . . inflatable car . . . inflatable fire extinguisher. I'm not even sure that works. . . ."

A massive wave of water crashed into the chamber, and pounded toward them.

"Hurry!" cried Smo.

"Ah, here it is, my inflatable dinghy!"

Donnie pulled the cord and they leaped aboard, just as the wave slammed down onto them.

CHAPTER THREE

THE SHAOLIN MONKEYS

Donnie was wrong. It wasn't Jet who had let go of his branch—it was Bruce. And not because he got bored, but because several small, hard objects had struck him in the back of the head. "OW!" he bellowed, falling to the ground.

"No!" cried Chuck, as Bruce's branch slotted back into position, and the door to the temple slammed shut.

"Nuts!" exclaimed Bruce.

Chuck and Jet dropped down beside him.

"What is it, Bruce?" asked Chuck.

Bruce rubbed his head and looked at the objects on the ground around him. "Nuts, like I said." He picked one up. "Someone's throwing nuts at us."

"Shaolin surprise!" cried a voice, as three monkeys sporting orange robes and spiky hairdos leaped out of the surrounding trees.

"I am Brother Bataar, and this is Turbold and Kamil," said the tallest of the three, nodding to the monkeys on his left and right. "We are the Shaolin Monkeys, protectors of this temple."

"Ha! You haven't done a very good job of protecting it! Two of our friends are already inside," Jet pointed out.

"Insolent mongoose!" cried the monkey named Turbold.

"Jet, be quiet," Chuck said. "We mean you no harm. We are merely here to—"

"Silence!" Brother Bataar commanded. "Shaolin troop, let us show them how we fight!"

Turbold aimed a flying kick at Jet, catching him off guard and sending him barging into Bruce. Jet sprang back onto his feet, responding with a cry of "Ninja-boom!" and a powerful roundhouse kick.

Turbold blocked Jet's attack and spun around to hit him again, but Jet ducked and rolled out of the way.

Nearby, Bruce took on Kamil, who seemed to have an endless supply of nuts, each nibbled into a sharp point. The monkey warrior threw them at the burly meerkat with the speed and force of bullets.

"Hey, stop that!" shouted Bruce.

"You cannot take it?" cried Kamil.

"No, I just think you're wasting perfectly good food," Bruce replied.

Meanwhile, Brother Bataar jumped up on his paws and catapulted himself at Chuck. Chuck bowed, so that the monkey flew straight over him. Then they both spun around and stood face to face.

"The ground you are standing on is ours," said Brother Bataar.

"Then I will take my leave," replied Chuck. He leaped into the air, twisting his body and swinging his tail at the monkey. Now it was Brother Bataar who had to dodge the attack. Chuck landed on the ground and aimed again, this time catching

the monkey's legs and bringing him crashing
down. Within seconds, Brother Bataar was
back on his feet and preparing to strike.

"Please, listen! We are here to protect
the Eye of the Monkey," said Chuck.

"As are we," replied Brother Bataar,
launching himself at Chuck once more.

Nearby, Turbold jumped in the air and
attempted to clap his paws around Jet's
head. Jet dodged and knocked Turbold
off his feet.

"I see you are familiar with the Drowned
Rat style of combat," said Jet.
"Unlike your hairdo, it's
very fashionable at the
moment."

WHAM!

"I am an expert in martial arts, but I do not care for fashion," replied Turbold. "Victory never goes out of style."

"Let's see how you look clothed in defeat," Jet snarled, attacking with his claws.

Turbold ducked. "Perhaps that's an outfit that would look better on you." He rolled into a ball and bowled himself at Jet, who jumped out of the way.

"I'm not sure how long we can go on like this," said Chuck, aiming a punch at his opponent.

"You are tired?" sneered Brother Bataar.

"No, but I can't listen to anymore battle banter from those two. Can we call a truce for a moment?"

Brother Bataar paused. "OK. Shaolin brothers, withdraw," he commanded. The other two monkeys jumped into formation behind him.

"You say you are the guardians of this temple," said Chuck. "Who gave you this great honor?"

"We are from a secret Shaolin temple in the Himalayas. For hundreds of years, our elders have picked the finest warriors to come here and stand guard over the temple and the precious Eye of the Monkey," Brother Bataar replied.

"Finest warriors, ha!" cried Jet.

Chuck shot Jet a warning glance. "Please continue," he urged Brother Bataar.

"We keep a constant watch over the entrance to the temple," the monkey explained.

"Then why did you allow my friends to enter before attacking?" asked Chuck.

"We knew that in dealing with you, the temple would eject them," replied Brother Bataar.

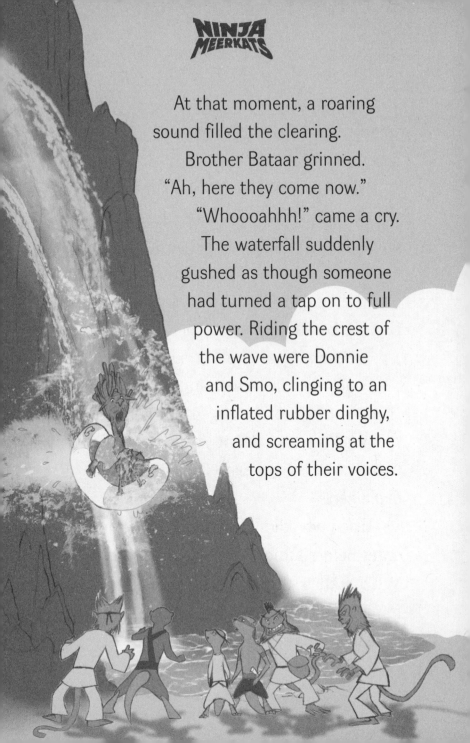

At that moment, a roaring
sound filled the clearing.
Brother Bataar grinned.
"Ah, here they come now."
"Whoooahhh!" came a cry.
The waterfall suddenly
gushed as though someone
had turned a tap on to full
power. Riding the crest of
the wave were Donnie
and Smo, clinging to an
inflated rubber dinghy,
and screaming at the
tops of their voices.

They crashed down into the pool below with a mighty splash, but soon surfaced and paddled to the shore.

"Now, that's what I call a ride!" said Donnie, climbing out of the dinghy and giving himself a good shake.

"I haven't had that much fun since I got lost in a field of sugarcane in Goa and had to eat my way out," Smo agreed.

Turbold gasped. "The Delhi Llama! I've read your book. You once beat the great bare-knuckle fighting bear of Bombay."

"Oh, he was just a teddy bear really," Smo said with a smile.

"You see, your friends have been successfully ejected. The Eye of the Monkey is impossible to steal," said Brother Bataar, bringing them back to the point.

But Donnie shook his head. "The jewel has gone."

"Impossible," said Kamil.

"We keep a constant watch from these trees and check on it every evening at dusk," said Brother Bataar.

"Well, someone has snuck in and taken it since you checked on it last, for I can confirm that the Eye is no longer there," said Smo. "You have my word as a disciple of the great Shaolin Monkey warrior, Brother Li-Luv that it was not us."

Brother Bataar bowed. "Then I believe you. But how is this possible?"

"You say you check on the jewel every evening," said Chuck. "What if the thief observed what you were doing? Could they have waited until after you had checked on the Eye, then entered the temple and taken it?"

"Impossible," said Turbold. "We would have seen them."

"But even if someone could have gotten in without us noticing, the Eye was kept well out of reach," said Brother Bataar.

"Donnie, did you find any clues inside the temple?" asked Chuck.

"There was a rope at the bottom of the statue in which the emerald was hidden," said Donnie.

"But the statue is designed to be unclimbable," said Kamil. "Everything slopes down—the ears, the nose—there is no way of attaching anything to it."

"Then, what was the rope used for?" asked Jet.

"I can think of only one answer: the Indian Rope Trick," Donnie replied.

"What's that?" asked Bruce.

"It's an amazing trick. A magician takes an ordinary rope, conjures it to stand on its end, then climbs up it," said Donnie.

"Oh, that sounds good. I like magic tricks," said Bruce. "My favorite is the one where they saw the lady in half."

"But the Indian Rope Trick is a myth," said Chuck. "No one has ever actually done it."

"Except for—" began Turbold.

"Hold your tongue," snapped Brother Bataar. "We will take our leave of you now."

"If you have a suspect in mind, you should tell us," said Chuck. "We could work together."

Brother Bataar shook his head. "This is a matter of pride for us. If the Eye has gone missing on our watch, we must retrieve it ourselves, otherwise we would never be able to show our faces in the Shaolin temple again. Shaolin Monkeys, come!" The three monkeys leaped into the trees and disappeared.

"Well, they seemed nice," said Bruce.

"Nice?" said Jet. "They just ambushed and attacked us, listened in on Donnie's ideas about the rope, and then ran off without telling us what they know."

"Yeah, but they had cool spiky hairdos and I liked their orange robes," said Bruce.

"The mention of the Indian Rope Trick clearly meant something to them," said Chuck. "Smo, have you any idea who could perform such a trick?"

"I'm afraid not, but I do know someone who might know," replied the llama. "He is my trusted contact in Agra—the one who informed me that someone had found out about the jewel's location in the first place."

"We must go to him at once," said Chuck. "Bruce, you come with me and Smo. Jet and Donnie—follow those monkeys."

CHAPTER FOUR

HERR FLICK

Donnie and Jet pursued Brother Bataar, Turbold, and Kamil on foot at first, taking care to stay hidden. The monkeys moved quickly, swinging from tree to tree out of the jungle, then jumping from rock to rock through the desert. When they reached Agra, they scampered up the sides of buildings and jumped across the rooftops.

"We're losing them," said Jet. "We might be quick, but we lack their climbing skills."

"Let's use the meerkite," said Donnie. From his backpack he pulled out a small glider, with two fold-out wings. He opened up the wings and slid the control bar into position. Then Jet grabbed hold of one end, and Donnie the other.

"Hang on tight!" Donnie cried, as they launched themselves off a rooftop. The wings caught a gust of wind and the two meerkats soared into the sky. Donnie angled the glider to the right to follow the monkeys. But as they did so, Jet noticed a huge circular red and black tent.

"It's the Ringmaster's big top," he said. "Let's take a closer look."

"But what about the monkeys?"

"We'll be able to see them for miles from up here, and catch up with them quickly," Jet assured him. "Anyway, if it *is* the Ringmaster who hired someone to steal the jewel, then we should definitely find out what he and his circus goons are up to."

"Good point." Donnie steered the glider lower to get a better view.

"Look, there's Sheffield and Grimsby," said Jet, spotting two sinister clowns patrolling the area.

"And Doris too," said Donnie, seeing the Ringmaster's faithful dancing dog coming out of the tent behind a tall blond man wearing a red shirt and a black vest. "But I don't recognize the guy she's with." The man had a belt full of knives strapped across his chest.

They swooped lower, circling the tip of the circus tent. "Hey, I wonder what's in those big trucks," Jet added, spotting two large trucks parked alongside the big top.

"Who knows, but we'd better get out of here before they spot us," Donnie whispered, making sure that their enemies below couldn't hear him.

Suddenly, there was the sound of dramatic music. "Oh no! That's my phone!" cried Donnie, fumbling to reach it.

But it was too late. The clowns looked up.

"Eh, Grimsby boy, what's got two tails and goes *arrrghh*?" said Sheffield.

"I don't know, what has two tails and goes *arrrghh*?" replied Grimsby.

"Those two meddlesome meerkats any second now." He turned to the man with the belt of knives. "Herr Flick, bring 'em down."

"With pleasure," replied the knife-thrower, speaking with a thick German accent. He selected a knife, took aim, and threw it. The knife spun through the air before slicing cleanly through the right wing of the glider, sending the meerkats spiralling to the ground.

Jet pulled out his nunchucks and swung at Doris, catching her nose as she leaped at them. She yelped in pain and fought back with a tango step, a growl, and a bite. Jet evaded her teeth, slid under her legs, grabbed her tail, and flung her into a large pile of elephant manure.

"Ha, the meerkätzchen threw the puppy into the poo poo," said the knife-thrower. "Now, it is *my* turn to cut in."

He drew two knives from his belt and flung them at Jet, who was forced to leap into a midair roll to avoid them.

Meanwhile, Donnie took on the clowns, both of whom had picked up huge rubber mallets. He dodged several blows, then whipped out a pair of handcuffs from his backpack and slapped them over the clowns' wrists. Sheffield lifted his mallet again, but as he did so he brought

Grimsby's weapon down onto his own head.

"Ow! Watch what you're doing with that," said Sheffield.

"No, you watch it," replied Grimsby, lifting his mallet and whacking himself in the head with Sheffield's.

With the two clowns occupied, Donnie was free to help Jet with Herr Flick. He delved into his backpack again and pulled out a large magnet. Then he hurried over to the nearest of the two trucks and hastily tied it to the front wheel. All of a sudden, the German knife-thrower found himself being dragged toward the magnet by his knife belt, and pinned to the truck.

"Nice one, Donnie," said Jet.

But the meerkats' moment of victory was short-lived as the back doors of both trucks crashed open. Two gigantic elephants stomped out of the darkness toward them, their trunks raised menacingly. Suddenly, two jets of water shot toward the meerkats, lifting them off their feet and knocking them out.

CHAPTER F1VE

AL1 UP

In another part of the city, Smo led Chuck and Bruce to the gates of the Taj Mahal. The area was full of tourists eager to have their photo taken in front of the famous monument. No one noticed the two meerkats and one limping llama who entered the lush gardens that stretched all the way to the temple. Chuck paused to admire the magnificent white building. "Humans are certainly capable of great things," he said.

"You're telling me. You should try this

chicken vindaloo with extra chili I found in the trash over there," said Bruce, licking his lips. "It's delicious!"

"I'm not sure a half-eaten curry really compares," said Chuck. "Smo, why are we here?"

"This is where my contact lives," the llama replied.

They had stopped near an old box with a sign on it which read DEAF, BLIND, AND LAME: PLEASE HELP. Next to the sign was an old hat with a couple of coins in it. Inside the box sat a sorry excuse for a dog. Half of its left ear was missing, one of its front legs was in a plaster cast, and it was wearing a pair of sunglasses.

A jolly American couple stopped to read the sign. "Hey, Herb, take a look at that cute little doggy," said the woman. "Give him some money, won't you?"

"Sure thing, poor little guy. Reminds me of old Tex back home," said her husband. He dropped a few coins into the hat as they walked past.

"Hi, Smo," said the dog, lifting off his sunglasses.

"Hey, you're not blind!" said Bruce.

"I'll have you know I have extremely sensitive eyes," the dog replied. He lifted his leg out of the plaster cast and scratched behind his good ear, then glanced at Bruce's curry. "That looks tasty," he said.

"Finders keepers!" said Bruce.

"Bruce, Chuck, this is Slumdoggy Dog," said Smo. "He knows everything that goes on in this city."

"I like to keep my ear to the ground," said the dog. "In fact, that's how I lost half of this one, a rickshaw ran over it. Still, it all helps with the look." He laughed wheezily. "So, what do you want to know?"

"Your lead was right," said Smo. "The Eye of the Monkey has been stolen, and the thief performed the Indian Rope Trick. Do you have any idea who that could be?"

"There's only one man in the whole of India who can do that," said Slum. "A magician called Ali Up. He's based in Agra."

"Sounds like our thief," said Chuck. "Where can we find him?"

"He has a theater in town," said Slum.

"Then we must pay him a visit," said Chuck. "I'll call Donnie and Jet to let them know to meet us there."

When neither Donnie nor Jet answered
their phones, Chuck left a message. Then
Slumdoggy Dog took them to Ali Up's
theater, which turned out to be a run-down
building in the middle of town. Outside, a
couple of men were putting up a sign that
read: ALI UP'S THEATER OF ILLUSION.
Standing below the sign, shouting up at
the men, was a short man with a neat
beard, wearing purple robes and a turban.

"A little up on the left," shouted the man. "That's good. This new sign should really draw in the crowds. Everyone will want to see the amazing Ali Up!"

"That's him," said Slum.

"Why is he talking about himself like he's somebody else?" asked Bruce.

"Sounds like he has a high opinion of himself," said Chuck.

"It is often the way with humans lacking in actual height," Smo observed.

"It's lucky that's not true of the animal kingdom, or we'd have an army of dormice set on taking over the world," said Slum. "Anyway, as much fun as it's been hanging out with you, I must be off. I don't want to miss out on this afternoon's tour buses."

"Thank you for your help," said Chuck.

"Anytime," Slum replied, with a wag of his tail. "See ya!"

As Slumdoggy Dog headed off, Chuck led the way around the side of the theater to a back door.

"Bruce and I will go inside and try to find out whether Ali Up still has the emerald. Smo, would you wait here in case the others arrive?"

"Of course," the llama replied.

Chuck and Bruce slipped through the door into the building. They made their way along the corridor to some steps that led to the side of the stage. Red cloth curtains with gold piping hung down from the ceiling and the whole stage was full of mirrors. Bruce looked at his reflection.

"Hey, look, Chuck, there are loads of me."

"After all that curry, there is indeed a lot of you," said Chuck, who was examining a plain red wardrobe in the center of the stage. "Ah, a vanishing box."

"A what?"

"A vanishing box. The magician shuts himself inside it, then, with a dramatic puff of smoke, he disappears."

They stepped inside the box to take a closer look.

"What does this lever do?" asked Bruce, reaching up to pull it.

"Don't do tha—"

There was a puff of smoke and the floor beneath their feet fell away. The two meerkats tumbled through the air and landed just in time to see a lid slam shut above them. They were trapped in a large box, the only light spilling in through some slits in the sides.

"What's going on?" Bruce roared.

"Who are you that would trespass on the property of the great Ali Up?" said a voice nearby. A human eye appeared at one of the slits. "Ah, the Clan of the Scorpion, I presume. The Ringmaster warned Ali Up that you might turn up. And you have fallen straight into Ali Up's trap!"

"You really do talk funny," growled Bruce.

"So you are another of the Ringmaster's hapless circus goons," said Chuck. "And the thief of the precious Eye of the Monkey."

"Ali Up works for no one but himself!" cried the magician. "The Ringmaster paid me to steal the jewel for him because he knew only Ali Up was *up* to such a task. And he will pay even more for this delivery than he did for the Eye."

"Not if I've got anything to do with it. Bruce Force!" Bruce cried. He thrust all his weight against the lid of the box, trying to push it off. But nothing he did had any effect.

Ali Up laughed. "You cannot escape. This box is sealed . . . just like your fates."

"For your own sake, I suggest you let us go. The Ringmaster is several cards short of a full deck and not someone you should deal with," said Chuck.

"No one tells Ali Up what to do," the magician replied. "I will take you to the Ringmaster's circus tent and see what he will pay for you."

CHAPTER SIX

RETURN OF THE LLAMA

Circus tents are supposed to be filled with eager spectators awaiting all kinds of exciting entertainment. But as the lights dimmed in the black-and-red striped tent on the outskirts of Agra, there was no audience to witness the imposing figure in the top hat step into the spotlight and raise the microphone to his lips. He tapped it twice before speaking. This was a dress rehearsal with a difference.

"Ladies and gentlemen, boys and girls..." The Ringmaster's voice echoed around the empty tent. "Tonight, for your viewing pleasure, we will amaze and delight you with some breathtaking feats. First up, a performer with four of them ... it's Doris the Dancing Dog!"

Doris fox-trotted into the central arena, dragging a bag that clanked behind her.

"Next ... they put the 'OW' into clown. It's Sheffield and Grimsby!"

The two clowns walked onto the stage, pushing an enormous wheel on a stand.

"Tonight, they'll be assisting a new member of our troupe. All the way from Berlin, Germany, and a cut above the rest— Herr Flick!"

Another spotlight revealed the knife-thrower, his daggers glinting menacingly.

"And let's not forget his two targets. For one night only—because that's as long as they'll last—Jet Flashfeet and

Donnie Dragonjab!"

The clowns turned the wheel around to reveal Jet and Donnie tied to opposite sides.

"You don't scare us," said Jet, trying to wriggle free.

Herr Flick threw his first dagger. It landed straight between Jet's legs.

"Speak for yourself," yelped Donnie.

The Ringmaster's laughter echoed around the empty tent. "Also . . . tonight's special guest. All the way from his theater across town, Agra's finest magician, Ali Up! He will be performing the Sword Box Illusion."

The bearded magician straightened his purple robes and strode onto the stage carrying a large box, which he placed on a table.

"Oh, that sounds fun," said Bruce's voice from inside the box.

"I suspect it will not be fun for *us*," replied Chuck's voice.

"Chuck! Bruce! Is that you?" cried Jet.

"I was hoping you two were going to turn up and rescue us," shouted Donnie.

"We were thinking the same thing about you," Chuck responded.

"Er, I tell you what, in a minute you meerkats are going to be like four little saints," said Sheffield.

"Four little saints?" asked Grimsby.

"Holy," said Sheffield. There was a
pause. "As in full of holes," he explained.

"Quiet!" snapped the Ringmaster.
He continued his announcement. "And
once we have rid ourselves of these
interfering meerkats, and with the Eye of
the Monkey in my possession, I will be
UNDEFEATABLE!" He laughed maniacally.
"Let's get on with the show. Ali Up, take
it away!"

"The great Ali Up will now thrust the
first sword into the box. . . ."

Doris fetched a sword from the bag she
had carried on stage. The magician chose
his spot, then plunged the weapon into
the box. . . .

At that precise moment, Donnie cried,
"Incoming, lengthways, down center!"

Inside
the box,
Chuck
and Bruce
dived out of the way,
just avoiding the blade
as it shot between them.

"Spin the wheel," cried the Ringmaster.
"That should keep Flashfeet and Dragonjab
out of trouble."

Sheffield and Grimsby turned the wheel
as fast as they could.

"Herr Flick, do your worst," exclaimed
the Ringmaster.

Herr Flick took aim. His cold, blue eyes
focused on the yellow blur of Jet's jumpsuit
as he spun around on the wheel.

"I forgot to mention that Herr Flick has
never missed a target," said the Ringmaster.

"That's good to know," said Jet.

There are some moments in life when all you can do is shut your eyes and hope for the best. One of these moments is when you find yourself tightly bound to a spinning wheel while an expert knife-thrower is aiming at your chest. And so Jet and Donnie shut their eyes and hoped for the best. But just as Herr Flick released his weapon, someone pushed him from behind. The knife veered off course, missing Jet's chest, but slicing through the rope that bound his right arm to the wheel. Quickly, he wriggled free. Now, to help the rest of the Clan!

"Ach, that is not fair! Someone pushed me!" complained Herr Flick. He turned around to find a dreadlocked llama behind him, his bad hind leg raised.

"Well, well, it turns out I can still do the Lightning Spin Kick." Smo Ka smiled.

"Smo!" cried Chuck from inside the box. "How did you find us?"

"When I saw Ali Up leave his theater, I guessed you were in the box he was carrying, and followed," Smo replied.

"The Delhi Llama," snarled the Ringmaster. "I might have known you'd be involved. Clowns, finish this old donkey."

As Sheffield and Grimsby approached, a voice behind them said, "I may have four hooves, but watch who you're calling a donkey."

They spun around. No one was there. Quick as a flash, Smo leaped into the air, spread his front two hooves and knocked the clowns unconscious.

BOFF!

"He's throwing his voice, you idiots!"
cried the Ringmaster. "Doris, get this lame
llama. And Ali Up, I'll double what
I'm paying you if you help."

HUMMM

Doris growled and stepped
forward. Balancing on his one
good hind leg, Smo made a
humming noise. Doris lunged
forward, but Smo hopped over
her head and landed on her
back, pinning Doris to the ground.
But the dancing dog was not finished
yet. She turned and bit down on Smo's
bad leg, making him cry out in pain. Ali Up
lunged towards the llama, and speedily
tied a rope to his weaker leg.

"No one gets the better of Ali Up!"
he cried. "*Shim shala bing!*" The rope
shot into the air, leaving Smo suspended
upside down.

"Hey, he raised the Smo Ka Llama," said Grimsby, coming to.

"Smoke alarm," chortled Sheffield. "Nice one, Grimsby."

Still dazed, the clowns tried to stand up, tripped over their own huge feet, and landed in a heap on the floor again.

The Ringmaster sighed. "Ladies and Gentlemen, please put your hands together for Ali Up and the legendary Indian Rope Trick," he announced.

"I'm sorry, my ninja friends," Smo sighed. "It seems my attempt to help has been suspended. As have I."

"Your bravery was not in vain, and the distraction was welcome," said Chuck. "We are ready to take back the jewel."

The Ringmaster spun around to find the four ninja meerkats standing behind him. A flicker of surprise crossed his face.

Then he said, "Ha! Come and get me!"

The meerkats bowed to each other.

"Before the Clan, each enemy cowers, for now we fight till victory is ours!" cried Chuck.

"All right," said Bruce. "Bruce Force!"

"Ninja-boom!" cried Jet.

The two meerkats flung themselves at the Ringmaster's chest . . . and bounced off him like two rubber balls off a brick wall.

BOING!

BOING!

"He has the protection of the jewel," said Smo. "He must have it on him now."

"The llama is right," exclaimed the Ringmaster. "I cannot be harmed. But the same cannot be said of you meerkats."

Herr Flick flung two knives at Chuck, who drew his sword and batted them away with lightning speed. The daggers sped on through the air, tearing through Ali Up's turban and one of his sleeves, and pinning him to the spinning wheel. "Release Ali Up at once!" the magician demanded.

"No matter what you throw at us, you shall not win," said Chuck.

"We'll see about that— bring in the heavies!" said the Ringmaster, cracking his whip.

The ground shook as two huge elephants stepped into the tent, their trunks raised.

"Behold! Two specially trained Indian elephants capable of shooting water from their trunks at thirty miles an hour," said the Ringmaster. "I call them my *Ele*phantastics!"

"He's not joking, Chuck," said Donnie. "These two dumbos knocked us out earlier."

"Quick! In front of the wheel," Chuck commanded. The meerkats leaped into position.

Chuck turned to the Ringmaster. "Now you cannot get us without also hitting Ali Up."

The Ringmaster threw back his head and laughed. "You think I care about this cheap conjuror? He has served his purpose. I have no further use for him. Elephantastics, knock them all out!"

CHAPTER SEVEN

SHAOLIN SURPRISE

As water blasted across the stage, the meerkats dived in different directions, leaving Ali Up to take the brunt of the powerful jets. The great wheel shattered into pieces under the force of the spray.

On the other side of the stage, the clowns had finally gotten to their feet. "Sheffield! Grimsby! Help the Elephantastics!" the Ringmaster ordered.

"We must split up," said Chuck. "Jet and Bruce, fend off the clowns. Donnie, find a way to stop the elephants' firing."

"I'm already on it," replied Donnie.

Jet and Bruce ran in opposite directions, barely managing to stay ahead of the gushing water as they battled the clowns. Chuck grabbed a piece of the wheel to use as a shield from Herr Flick's flying knives.

Protected behind Chuck's shield, Donnie pulled a device made out of old tin cans from his backpack.

"I call this my bazoo-CAN," he said. "I just need some ammunition the right size to block those trunks."

At that moment, two large nuts, nibbled into the shape of bullets, dropped from the ceiling and landed at Donnie's feet. "What the . . . ?" said Donnie, picking them up. He and Chuck raised their heads and saw the three Shaolin Monkeys climbing in through the hole in the center of the tent's roof.

"Shaolin surprise!" cried Turbold, dropping down onto Sheffield's shoulders and bashing his ears.

The Ringmaster roared with anger.

"We are the Shaolin Monkeys and we are here to return the Eye to its rightful place," screeched Brother Bataar, knocking Grimsby to the floor.

"Elephantastics, aim at those gate-crashing monkeys!" yelled the Ringmaster.

"Catch us if you can," goaded Kamil.

"Donnie, I believe it is time to pack their trunks," said Chuck.

"Just what I was thinking," replied Donnie. He loaded the nuts into the bazoo-CAN, stepped out from behind the shield, took aim, and fired.

The nuts cut through the air with terrifying speed, zoomed through the water jets, and up the elephants' trunks. Instantly, the flow of water stopped. The elephants blew harder, trying to get rid of the blockage, but their trunks merely swelled up. Then they both turned an alarming shade of red and passed out with two earth-shaking thuds.

WHOOSH!

"Nooo! My Elephantastics!" the Ringmaster bellowed. "The rest of you—wipe out these monkeys and extinguish these meerkats!"

The ninja meerkats and Shaolin Monkeys were now fighting side by side. Brother Bataar got hold of Doris's tail while Bruce grabbed her by the collar, and together they flung her into the clowns.

"Get the Ringmaster," ordered Chuck. "He has the Eye."

Kamil grabbed a handful of nuts from his pouch. He shoved them into his mouth and fired them at the Ringmaster, but each one bounced off without making the slightest impact.

The Ringmaster laughed, a mad glint in his eye.

Smo, who was still hanging upside down at the top of the rope, cried out, "Warriors! No weapon can harm he who holds the Eye of the Monkey. The only way is to part the man from the jewel."

"But where is it?" said Jet.

"I believe that, like most people with secrets, he is keeping this one very much under his hat," replied Smo.

"Curse you, you old fool," cried the Ringmaster, cracking his whip across Smo's back.

"Hey, you can't do that to the Delhi Llama," snarled Jet. "You'll pay for that." With the other meerkats busy fighting the rest of the circus, he turned to Turbold and whispered, "Prepare to grab the jewel."

"But how? The Eye will protect him

from any attack," replied Turbold.

"Not one that isn't intended to hurt him," said Jet. "One, two, three . . . Ninja-boom!"

Moving faster than the blink of an eye, Jet leaped high in the air, and for the first time ever, performed the legendary Lightning Spin Kick, knocking the Ringmaster's hat off his head. Before he had time to react, Turbold leapfrogged over the Ringmaster's head, grabbing the exposed jewel as he went.

"Shaolin-boom!" he cried, holding the Eye up in the air.

"Hey, keep your monkey paws off my catchphrase," protested Jet.

"Circus troupe, catch that monkey!" bellowed the Ringmaster. "He has the Eye!" Herr Flick turned and flung a knife at Turbold. It bounced off him and the Ringmaster had to duck to avoid it.

"The monkey can't be harmed, you idiots," he said. "You have to take the stone from him."

Faithful as ever, Doris leaped up and snatched the jewel in her teeth.

"Good dog, Doris," said the Ringmaster.

"Oh no, you don't," yelled Bruce. He launched himself at her . . . and bounced straight off again. However, his attack distracted Doris long enough for Donnie

to grab his fishing rod device and yank the Eye from her jaws.

"I'll have that!" he cried.

But before he even had the emerald in his paws, Ali Up—who had finally recovered from his drenching—staggered to his feet and used one of his swords to slice through the fishing line and seize the jewel.

"Now, the Eye is back with the great
Ali Up," he cried.

"Good work, Ali," said the Ringmaster. He
held out his hand. "Now, give it to me."

"The Ringmaster has already betrayed
you once," said Chuck. "Don't let him do
it again."

"Ignore him," said the Ringmaster.
"I was the one who told you where the
stone was, and do not forget I have
already paid you for it. Now,
hand it over."

"The Eye was never yours
to sell, Mr. Up," said Chuck.
"You already made the wrong
choice in using your magical abilities
to steal it for this villain. Now, it is
time to make the right choice."

"The great Ali Up only wanted
money to repair his theater," the
magician replied. "Ali Up never
wanted anyone to get hurt!"

"Give me the Eye,"
demanded the Ringmaster.

The magician pulled himself up to his full height, which was still not very tall. "No one tells the great Ali Up what to do!" he said. "It is time for me to go. *Shim shala bing.*"

Ali Up waved his hands dramatically and vanished in a puff of smoke.

"Quickly, all of you, after him," said the Ringmaster. "He can't have gotten far."

The Ringmaster and his circus goons sped out of the tent.

"We must follow!" said Chuck. "We cannot allow the Ringmaster to get his hands on the jewel again."

"Wait," whispered Brother Bataar, placing a paw on Chuck's arm. "It seems your words convinced the magician to do the right thing."

"But he has vanished with the stone," said Chuck.

"No. He has gone but look, he has left the Eye." Brother Bataar lowered his arm and the emerald rolled out of his robe.

"Talk about keeping something up your sleeve!" said Jet.

"Now, that's what I call magic," said Bruce.

"I have to say, you meerkats fought well," said Kamil.

"I couldn't have stopped those elephants without your help," admitted Donnie.

"And I am in awe of your ability to perform the Lightning Spin Kick, Jet Flashfeet," said Turbold.

"I couldn't have done it without the inspiration of the great Delhi Llama," said Jet.

"Oh, remembered me, have you?" said Smo, still hanging upside down from the rope. "Perhaps you would be so kind as to GET ME DOWN!"

CHAPTER EIGHT

THE INDIAN ROPE TRICK

The four meerkats and Smo Ka watched as the sun set behind the Taj Mahal. The Clan of the Scorpion had bid farewell to the Shaolin Monkeys and the Eye of the Monkey outside the big top. They had then scoured the city for the Ringmaster, but he and his circus troupe had disappeared without a trace.

"Will the monkeys return the Eye to the temple, do you think?" asked Jet.

"No, it is no longer safe there," said Chuck. "The temple's secrecy was its

best form of security. They will take it
to a new hidden location."

"Where's that then?" asked Bruce, who
was tucking into a chicken korma.

"It's a secret, Bruce," said Donnie. "That's
the point."

"Oh. Right," he said.

"What will happen to Ali Up?" asked Jet.

"Yeah, I liked him," said Bruce.

"Bruce, he trapped you in a box and tried
to skewer you with swords," said Donnie.

"I know, but he did the right thing in
the end," said Bruce, his mouth full.

"Ali Up will not be able to return to his
theater for fear that the Ringmaster will
find him," said Chuck. "But I daresay he
will continue to work as a magician
elsewhere."

"He should be behind bars, not on
stage," said Jet.

"It's hard to imprison a man who can disappear in a puff of smoke!" said Smo. "And even though I was on the wrong end of it, I was still impressed that he could perform the Indian Rope Trick."

"I can do that, no problem," said Donnie. "Watch this." He pulled out a piece of rope from his backpack. "*Sham shala bong!*"

The rope shot up straight in the air.

"Very clever, Donnie," said Chuck. "But can you climb it now?"

"I'll do it," said Jet, leaping up.

"That's not a good idea—"

But Jet had already grabbed the rope and started climbing. All of a sudden, the rope wobbled, then collapsed, and Jet tumbled down, landing headfirst in the middle of Bruce's curry.

"Ninja-*bhuna*!" cried Jet, bursting out laughing and wiping curry sauce from his eye.

"I don't see what's so funny about you spilling my chicken korma," Bruce said sulkily.

"Come on, it's only a curry," said Donnie. "You should *korma* down."

"Oh well, at least you had rice with it," said Chuck, looking at Bruce with a smile. "It means Jet had a soft *pilau* to land on."

The others groaned.

"Come on, Bruce," said Jet. "I'll find you another curry. We've got to keep your strength up. After all, who knows when our next adventure will come along!"

CHUCK
COBRACRUSHER

Leader of the Clan
(and the brains)

Specialist ninja skill:
Nifty with the sword
Most likely to be heard saying:
Before the Clan, each enemy cowers,
for now we fight till victory is ours!
Most likely to be found:
Meditating or practicing his sword-play
(though not at the same time)
Famous for:
Remaining calm under pressure

JET
FLASHFEET

Superfast ninja
A lean, mean, fighting machine

Specialist ninja skill:
A sure hand with the nunchucks
Most likely to be heard saying:
Ninja-boom!
Most likely to be found:
Practicing his moves and reading his collection of magazines and books. His favorites are *What Karate!*, *101 More Martial Arts Moves*, and *Kung Fu Weekly*
Famous for:
His impetuous ways, which can lead to trouble...

NINJA MEERKATS

BRUCE
WILLOWHAMMER

aka Bruce "the muscle" Willowhammer

The clue's in the name, this fella is a mighty powerhouse of strength

Specialist ninja skill:
The throw–anytime, any place, anywhere…anyone…

Most likely to be heard saying:
Time for some Bruce Force!

Most likely to be found:
Doing 100 push-ups while planning a BIG breakfast

Famous for:
His bottomless appetite

NINJA MEERKATS

DONNIE
DRAGONJAB

Brilliant inventor
and master of gadgets

Specialist ninja skill:
Being able to turn anything into
a deadly weapon
Most likely to be heard saying:
Something sarcastic
Most likely to be found:
Taking things apart, putting things
back together, and devising cunning
disguises
Famous for:
His love of technology

NINJA
MEERKATS

Grandmaster One-Eye has been kidnapped and taken to an icy fortress! The Meerkats are in hot pursuit, but can the Grandmaster be found before the trail runs cold?

Find out what happens in
Ninja Meerkats:
Escape from Ice Mountain.

CHAPTER ONE

THE GRANDMASTERS' REUNION

The pilot of the twin-engine plane looked down at the Chilean mountain range. Even in the fading evening light, he could see all the way down to the southernmost tip of South America.

But what he failed to see were five small furry stowaways jumping out of his plane and parachuting down to earth. Chuck Cobracrusher, Donnie Dragonjab, Jet Flashfeet, and Bruce Willowhammer were all using parachutes designed by Donnie, with toggles on either side allowing them to steer.

Bruce was having the most difficulty, as he had their ancient mentor, Grandmaster One-Eye, strapped to his back.

"What are we aiming for?" shouted Jet, pulling his right toggle and swooping around in front of the others.

"The ground," smirked Donnie.

"We are aiming for the Academy of Revered Grandmasters, for Grandmaster One-Eye's school reunion," Chuck yelled over the sound of rushing wind.

"Did you really go to school here, Grandmaster?" asked Bruce.

Grandmaster One-Eye nodded.

"It seems like a long way to travel every day from the Red Desert," said Bruce.

"Bruce, the students who attend the ARG *live* at the academy," said Chuck.

"So, where is this place, Grandmaster?" asked Bruce. "I can't see it yet."

"I'm afraid I cannot see it either," replied One-Eye.

"Bruce, remember that Grandmaster One-Eye's eyesight is not as good as yours," Chuck pointed out.

"It isn't that," said One-Eye. "I've had my eyes shut since we jumped out of the plane. If meerkats were meant to see the world from such heights, they would have wings."

"My granddad had wings," said Bruce.

"No, he didn't," sighed Donnie.

"Yes, he did. I never saw them myself, but I remember Mom saying she wouldn't have him in the burrow because he had such a bad case of wings."

"I think that would have been *wind*," said Jet.

"Oh. That does make more sense now that you say it," admitted Bruce.

"Follow me," said Chuck,
pulling his toggles and aiming
for a spot near the top of a hill.
When he was moments from
the ground, he released the
parachute and landed into a roll.
The others followed suit, except
for Bruce, who took the force of
the landing in his knees to
avoid flattening Grandmaster
One-Eye. In front of them
were two large wooden
gates. A long golden rope
hung to one side.

"Ah, now this brings back memories," said Grandmaster One-Eye as Bruce set him on the ground. "Would you give me a moment before we go any farther?"

"You need time to reflect on all that has happened since you were last here?" said Chuck.

"No, I drank rather a lot of tea while we were waiting for that plane to take off and I need the bathroom," said Grandmaster One-Eye.

Jet chuckled and the Grandmaster disappeared into a nearby bush.

"Bruce, keep an eye on him," said Chuck.

"What? Watch him go to the toilet?" exclaimed Bruce.

"Yes. The last time he went, we lost him for an hour," replied Chuck.

"Don't worry," replied Donnie. "I've attached a tracking device to his robe so there's no chance of losing him again."

"I'm looking forward to getting inside and having some grub," said Bruce, carefully watching the bush Grandmaster One-Eye was hidden behind. "Oooh, I used to love school dinners. Mealworm mash, mealworm stew, mealworm Bolognaise . . ."

"We will not be entering the grounds," said Chuck. "According to ancient ninja code, no one is allowed to walk into the temple without an invitation."

"So, no mealworms?" said Bruce, disappointed.

"Not unless you find them yourself. We will set up camp nearby," said Chuck. "After the reunion, we will accompany Grandmaster One-Eye back home."

"I wish we could get inside and take a sneak peek," said Jet. "The ARG is the coolest academy in the world." He scurried onto a rock and jumped up, trying to see over the wall, but it was far too high.

"Please remove yourself from my shell," said a voice.

"Who said that?" asked Jet, spinning around.

"It was that rock you're standing on," said Donnie.

"That is no rock," said Chuck. "Jet, climb down at once."

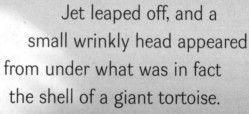

Jet leaped off, and a small wrinkly head appeared from under what was in fact the shell of a giant tortoise.

GOFISH

Gareth P. Jones

What did you want to be when you grew up?
At various points, a writer, a musician, an intergalactic bounty hunter and, for a limited period, a graphic designer. (I didn't know what that meant, but I liked the way it sounded.)

When did you realize you wanted to be a writer?
I don't remember realizing it. I have always loved stories. From a very young age, I enjoyed making them up. As I'm not very good at making things up on the spot, this invariably involved having to write them down.

What's your most embarrassing childhood memory?
Seriously? There are too many. I have spent my entire life saying and doing embarrassing things. Just thinking about some of them is making me cringe. Luckily, I have a terrible memory, so I can't remember them all, but no, I'm not going to write any down for you. If I did that, I'd never be able to forget them.

SQUARE FISH

What's your favorite childhood memory?
To be honest with you, I don't remember my childhood very well at all (I told you I had a bad memory), but I do recall how my dad used to tell me stories. He would make them up as he went along, most likely borrowing all sorts of elements from the books he was reading without me knowing.

As a young person, who did you look up to most?
My mom and dad, Prince, Michael Jackson, all of Monty Python, and Stephen Fry.

What was your favorite thing about school?
Laughing with my friends.

What was your least favorite thing about school?
I had a bit of a hard time when I moved from the Midlands to London at the age of twelve because I had a funny accent. But don't worry, it was all right in the end.

What were your hobbies as a kid? What are your hobbies now?
I love listening to and making music. My hobbies haven't really changed over the years, except that there's a longer list of instruments now. When I get a chance, I like idling away the day playing trumpet, guitar, banjo, ukulele, mandolin (and piano if there's one in the vicinity). I also like playing out with my friends.

What was your first job, and what was your "worst" job?

My first job was working as a waiter. That's probably my worst job, too. As my dad says, I was a remarkably grumpy waiter. I'm not big on all that serving-people malarkey.

What book is on your nightstand now?

I have a pile of books from my new publisher. I'm trying to get through them before I meet the authors. I'm half-way through *Maggot Moon* by Sally Gardner, which is written in the amazing voice of a dyslexic boy.

How did you celebrate publishing your first book?

The first time I saw one of my books in a shop, I was so excited that I caused something of a commotion. I managed to persuade an unsuspecting customer to buy it so I could sign it for her son.

Where do you write your books?

Anywhere and everywhere. Here are some of the locations I have written the Ninja Meerkats series: On the 185 and the 176 buses in London, various airplanes, Hong Kong, Melbourne, all over New Zealand, a number of cafes and bars between San Diego and San Francisco, New Quay in South Wales, and my kitchen.

What sparked your imagination for the Ninja Meerkats?

The idea came from the publishing house, but from the moment I heard it, I really wanted to write it. It reminded me of lots of action-packed cartoons I used to watch when I was young. I love the fact that I get to cram in lots of jokes and puns, fast action, and crazy outlandish plots.

The Ninja Meerkats are awesome fighters; have you ever studied martial arts? If so, what types?
Ha, no. If I was to get into a fight, my tactic would be to fall over and hope that whoever was attacking me lost interest.

If you were a Ninja Meerkat, what would your name be?
Hmm, how about Gareth *POW!* Jones?

What's your favorite exhibit or animal at the zoo?
Funnily enough, I like the meerkats. I was at a zoo watching them the other day when it started to rain. They suddenly ran for cover, looking exactly like their human visitors.

What's Bruce's favorite food?
Anything with the words ALL YOU CAN EAT written above it.

If you had a catchphrase like Bruce Force! or Ninja-Boom! what would it be?
That's a tricky one. How about PEN POWER!

If you were a Ninja Meerkat, what would your special ninja skill be?
I like to think I'd be like Jet, and always working on a new one. When I got into school, I took the Random Move

Generator! We used it to come up with new moves, like the Floating Butterfly Punch and the Ultimate Lemon Punch.

What is your favorite thing about real-life meerkats? Have you ever met a meerkat?
I was lucky enough to go into a meerkat enclosure recently. They were crawling all over me, trying to get a good view. It was brilliant.

In *The Eye of the Monkey* the Meerkats travel to India, have you ever been to India?
I went to India for three months when I finished college. It was an amazing experience. I traveled all over, met lots of interesting people, and got so ill that I came back as thin as a rake.

What challenges do you face in the writing process, and how do you overcome them?
The challenge with writing the Ninja Meerkats books is mostly about the plotting. It's trying to get all the twists and turns to work, and to avoid them feeling predictable. When I hit problems, I write down as many options as I can think of from the completely ordinary to utterly ridiculous. Once they're all down on paper, the right answer normally jumps out at you.

Which of your characters is most like you?
I'd like to say that I'm wise and noble like Chuck, but I'm probably more like the Ringmaster as we're both always coming up with new ways to take over the world.

What makes you laugh out loud?
My friends.

What do you do on a rainy day?
Play guitar, write, watch TV, or go out with my sword-handled umbrella.

What's your idea of fun?
Answering questionnaires about myself. Actually, to-morrow, I'm going to a music festival with my wife where we will dance and cavort. That should be fun.

What's your favorite song?
There are far too many to mention, but today I think I'll go for "Feel Good Inc." by Gorillaz.

Who is your favorite fictional character?
Another tricky one, but today I'll say Ged from the Earth-sea Trilogy by Ursula K. Le Guin.

What was your favorite book when you were a kid? Do you have a favorite book now?
As a child, I especially loved *The Phantom Tollbooth* by Norton Juster.

What's your favorite TV show or movie?
Raiders of the Lost Ark.

If you were stranded on a desert island, who would you want for company?
My wife and son, then probably my friend Pete, as he's really handy and would be able to make and build things.

If you could travel anywhere in the world, where would you go and what would you do?
I'd like to go to Canada next. Ideally, I'd like to go and live there for a bit. I've never been to South America. There are also lots of parts of America I haven't visited yet.

If you could travel in time, where would you go and what would you do?
I think I'd travel to the future and see what's changed and whether anyone's invented a new kind of umbrella.

What's the best advice you have ever received about writing?
Don't tell the story, show the story.

What do you consider to be your greatest accomplishment?
Getting published and getting married.

What do you wish you could do better?
Draw.

What would your readers be most surprised to learn about you?
I'm writing this while working as a TV producer, sitting in a hot editing suite, pretending I'm working hard.

 SQUARE FISH